The GARDEN TROLL

Vicki C. Hayes

red rhino books™

Body Switch
Clan Castles
The Code
Fish Boy
Flyer
Fight School
The Garden Troll
Ghost Mountain
The Gift
The Hero of Crow's Crossing
I Am Underdog
Killer Flood
Little Miss Miss
The Lost House
The Love Mints
Out of Gas
Racer
Sky Watchers
Standing by Emma
Starstruck
Stolen Treasure
The Soldier
Too Many Dogs
Zombies!
Zuze and the Star

With more titles on the way ...

ISBN-13: 978-1-62250-916-4
ISBN-10: 1-62250-916-1
eBook: 978-1-63078-044-9

Printed in Guangzhou, China
NOR/0215/CA21500098

19 18 17 16 15   1 2 3 4 5

Garden Troll

Age: Really, really, *really* old

Favorite Foods: Rotten leaves and dry twigs

Greatest Fear: The wizard

Future Goal: To cause lots more trouble

Best Quality: Hosts his brother's birthday party every year

Age: 12

Special Skill: Can wiggle her ears

Most Private Secret: Actually glad her dad married Ellen

Future Goal: To own a horse farm in Oregon

Best Quality: Knows when she is wrong

1
THE WISH

Jenny was in trouble again. It didn't matter what the twelve-year-old did. She couldn't please her stepmom, Ellen.

"I did clean my room," said Jenny.

"Yes," said Ellen. "But you left dirty dishes under your bed."

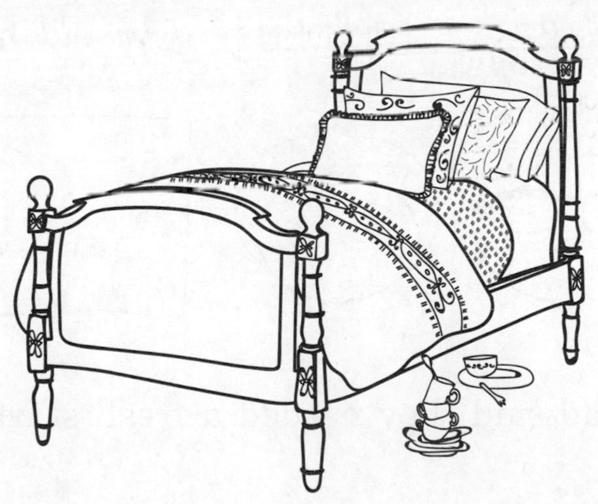

"I did fill the dishwasher," said Jenny.

"Yes," said Ellen. "But you forgot to start it. You need to take a little more care."

"Leave me alone," yelled Jenny.

Jenny stomped out the back door. She hated Ellen. She hated this old house. She was happy with Dad. She was happy with her little brother, Nick. She was happy with their other house. Then Dad had to go and marry Ellen. Their mom had been dead a long time. But still …

Dad said they needed a fresh start. He

said they needed a new house. He said Ellen liked this house. Ellen was an artist. She said the house was charming. Dad agreed with Ellen. Even Nick liked the house. But Jenny didn't. The house wasn't charming. It was old. And it was ugly. Even the yard was a mess.

← These weeds are everywhere!

Jenny walked to the back of the yard. There was an old garden. It was full of weeds. It was full of stones. It looked the way Jenny felt. It looked sad and messed up.

The stone walls were mostly gone. There

was one stone post left. It was four feet high. And covered with ivy. On top sat a little stone man. He had a round tummy. He wore baggy pants. And a floppy hat. Jenny thought he looked like a troll. He was frowning. Jenny thought he looked funny.

"You are the only thing I like," said Jenny. "You are the only thing I like about this old place."

Jenny patted the troll's head. "I don't like this house. I don't like this yard. And I don't like Ellen," Jenny told the troll.

The troll didn't say anything. Jenny liked that. She traced his frown with her finger. "I'm always in trouble," Jenny said. "It's not fair. I wish Ellen would get in trouble!"

Suddenly the troll felt hot. Jenny pulled her hand away. She stared at the troll. But he looked the same. Did he really get hot? Jenny touched the troll again. Then she heard a voice.

2
THE TROLL

"Hey," said the voice. "What are you doing?" It was Nick. He was coming across the yard. He was kicking his soccer ball.

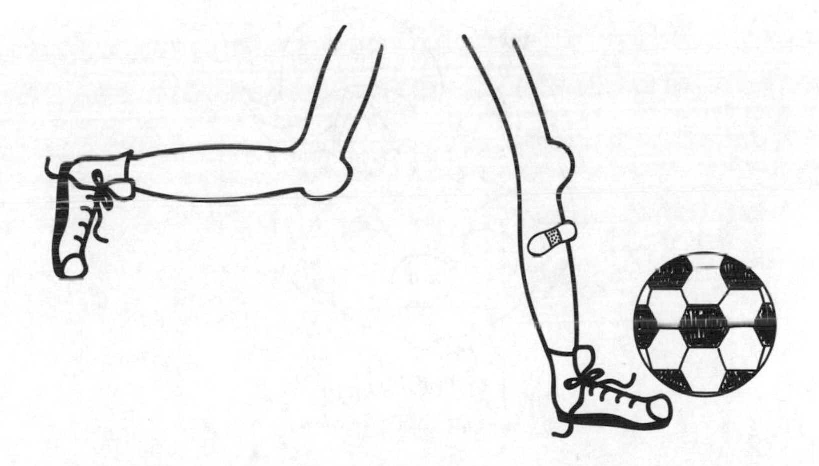

"Nothing," said Jenny. She let go of the troll.

"Cool troll," said Nick. "Isn't this a rad garden?" He joined her by the stone post.

"It's old and messy," said Jenny.

"Yeah," said Nick. "But I like it. I like the house too. It's charming."

Jenny snorted. "You heard Ellen say that," she said. "That's not a Nick word. You always copy Ellen." Jenny started to walk away.

"What's wrong with Ellen?" asked Nick. "She's nice. I like her."

"It was better before," said Jenny. "When there were just three of us. You don't remember it."

"I do too," said Nick. "But I like having Ellen in the family. You need to give her a chance. Will you help me with my soccer kicks?"

"Fine," said Jenny. She liked her brother. She didn't like Ellen.

Jenny and Nick kicked the soccer ball back and forth. Then Nick gave a really hard kick. The ball went toward the stone post. It hit the post hard. The post shook back and forth.

"Watch out," yelled Jenny. "You might break something." She went to look at the troll. She didn't want him broken.

"Nick, come here!" Jenny called.

"What's wrong?" said Nick. "Is he broken?"

"Look at the troll," said Jenny. "He's changed."

Nick came over to the post. He looked at the troll.

Something's different ...

"I think he looks okay," said Nick.

"No," said Jenny. "He was frowning before. Now he's grinning."

"I don't think so," said Nick. "Anyway, how could he change his face?"

Jenny didn't answer. She heard the sound of a car. It pulled into the driveway.

"It's Dad," yelled Nick. He ran to the front yard. Jenny followed.

"Hey, Nick," said Dad. He got out of the car. "How was your day?"

"Great!" said Nick. "I got on a soccer team."

"Good job," said Dad. "How was your day, Jenny?"

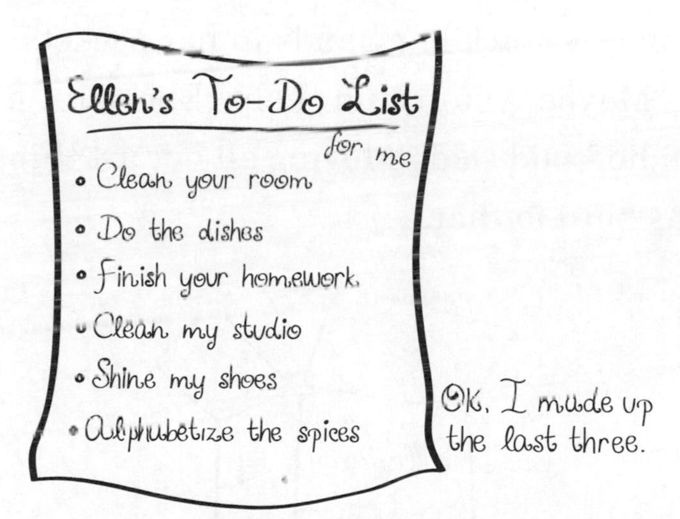

"No fun," said Jenny. "Ellen kept yelling at me. I had to clean my room. I had to help with the dishes. I had to do my homework. I hate Ellen."

Dad frowned.

"I don't like you saying that," he said. "You need to try to get along. These changes are hard for Ellen too."

Jenny kicked some stones in the driveway.

"Please try," said Dad.

Jenny stuck her hands in her pockets.

"Maybe you could help Ellen in her studio," said Dad. "Moving all her art things was hard for her."

Jenny didn't look at Dad.

"Jenny?" said Dad.

"Okay," said Jenny. "I'll think about it."

Me, thinking of other things

Dad sighed. He went in the house.

Jenny and Nick walked to the backyard. Nick began kicking his soccer ball again. Jenny joined him. But then she remembered the troll. Had its face really changed? She looked at the stone post. Something was wrong.

"Nick! Come quick!" she yelled.

"What is it?" asked Nick. "Is the troll frowning or grinning?" He kicked his ball toward the old garden.

Jenny was staring at the post. Nick looked up at the troll. His eyes opened wide. The troll wasn't frowning. The troll wasn't grinning.

Why?

The troll wasn't there!

3
TROUBLE

"He's gone!" said Jenny.

"He probably fell off," said Nick. "My soccer ball banged the post pretty hard. Look on the ground."

Jenny frowned. Had the troll fallen off? She wasn't sure. She looked on the ground. She looked around the post. She even looked in the ivy. But no troll.

"Dinner!" called a voice. It was Ellen.

The kids went inside. They sat at the table with Ellen and Dad.

Dad passed the salad. "What have you been doing?" he asked.

"Nothing," said Jenny.

"Yes we were," said Nick. "We were looking for … ouch!" Jenny kicked Nick's leg. He looked at her. She was frowning.

"We were looking for Nick's ball," said Jenny. "It went into the old garden."

"Did you find it?" asked Dad.

"Yes," said Nick. Then he started talking about his new soccer team.

After dinner, Jenny pulled Nick to the back porch.

"You can't tell them about the troll," said Jenny. "They wouldn't understand."

"You're right," said Nick. "They will think you're crazy."

"Please," said Jenny. "Help me find him."

Nick sighed. "Okay," he said. "Let's go back to the garden. We can look around some more."

Jenny and Nick stepped off the porch. They walked to the old garden.

"Look," said Nick. "The troll is on the post. Are you playing a joke?" He turned to his sister. He looked mad.

"No," said Jenny. "I didn't put him there. This is very strange." She reached up. She tried to pull the troll off the post. But it wouldn't move.

"Well, someone did," said Nick. He started back to the house. Jenny stared at the troll. Then she turned and followed Nick.

"Are you ready for dessert?" asked Ellen when the kids came in. "I made a surprise."

"Sure," said Nick. "What is it?"

"Ice cream cake," said Ellen. She opened the freezer. "Oh no," said Ellen.

Dad came in the kitchen. "What's the matter?" he asked.

"The freezer is off," said Ellen. "My surprise has melted."

Dad looked at the freezer.

"Here's the problem," he said. "The plug

is out." Dad put the plug back in the wall. But it was too late. The cake had melted.

"It's too soft to eat," said Ellen. "I'm sorry, everyone."

"That's okay," said Nick. "I'll eat it anyway."

"Me too," said Dad. "It will taste like a milkshake." He looked at Jenny.

"Yes, I'll eat it too," said Jenny. But she was thinking about the troll.

Later that evening, Dad came into Jenny's room. He came to say good night.

"Have a good sleep," he said.

"Thanks, Dad," said Jenny. He gave her a kiss. He turned to leave the room. Then he stopped.

"Jenny," he said. "I was wondering about the freezer plug. Do you know how it came out?"

"No," said Jenny. She looked at Dad with surprise.

"Okay," he said. "But you were mad with Ellen before."

"I wouldn't ruin dessert," said Jenny. "I bet the plug was kicked out by mistake."

"Maybe," said Dad. "But I don't see how." He gave Jenny another kiss and left.

Jenny slipped out of bed. She crept into Nick's room.

"Nick," said Jenny softly.

"Hmm?" said Nick from his bed.

"Nick, I think the troll did it."

"Did what?" asked Nick.

"Unplugged the freezer," said Jenny.

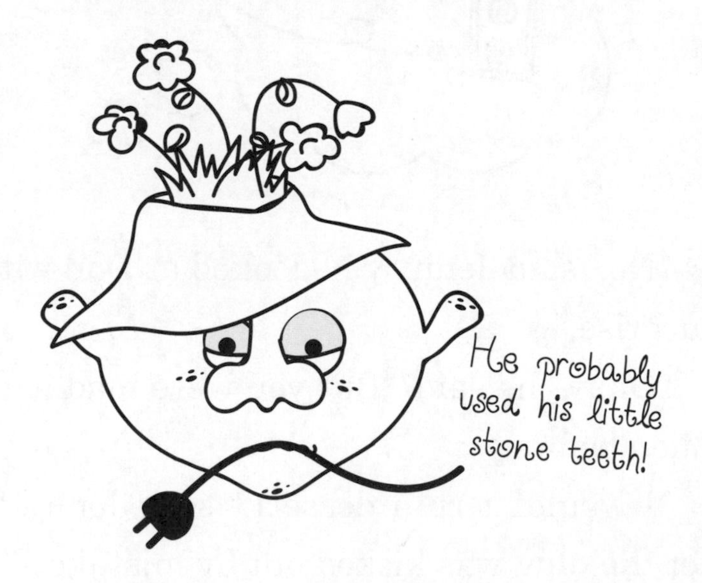

"Why would the troll do that?" asked Nick.

"Because I asked him to," said Jenny. "I made a wish."

"You're crazy," said Nick. "Go back to bed."

Jenny looked at her brother. Maybe he was right. How could a stone troll grant wishes? She must be crazy. Jenny went back to her room. But it took a while before she fell asleep. She was still thinking about the troll.

4
LITTER

Jenny walked into the kitchen. The bright sun hurt her eyes. She plopped down on a chair.

"Good morning," said Ellen. She was packing lunches for Nick and Jenny. "Jenny, do me a favor. Please."

"Okay," said Jenny. She put corn flakes and milk in a bowl.

"Please drag the trash cans to the curb," said Ellen. "Today is trash day."

Jenny nodded. Her mouth was full of corn flakes.

After eating, Jenny went out. She grabbed the two trash cans. She dragged them to the curb. Next she went to the garden. She wanted to check on the troll. Then she came back in. Nick and Dad were eating.

"Our friend is gone again," Jenny said to Nick.

"What friend?" asked Dad.

"Someone Nick and I met," said Jenny. "He likes to play tricks."

"That doesn't sound very friendly," said Dad.

Nick got up from the table.

"Where are you going?" asked Dad. "You need to finish your food."

"I want to go outside," said Nick.

"Not till you're done," said Dad.

Nick sat back down. He gulped his food. "I'm done," he said. He jumped up. He ran out the back door.

"I'm off to work," said Dad. He gave Jenny a hug. "Have a good day at school."

Ellen said goodbye to Jenny. Then she walked out with Dad.

Nick came back into the kitchen. He put his hands on his hips. He looked mad.

“He is not gone,” said Nick.

“What?” said Jenny. But then Ellen came back in.

“I can’t start the car,” said Ellen. “I have to go to an art show. The car must be fixed. I’m going to call someone to fix it.” Ellen got on the phone.

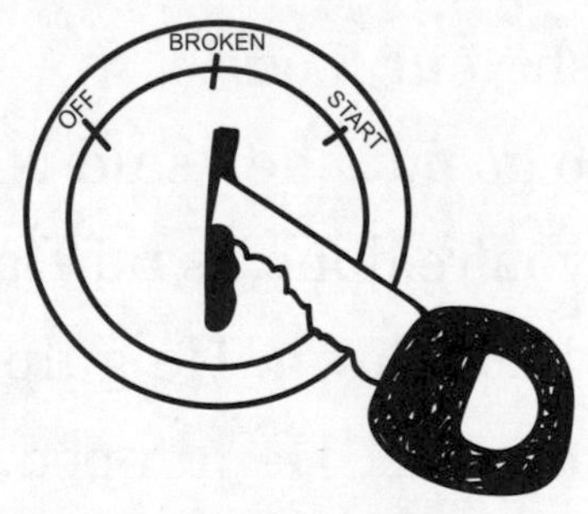

Jenny looked at Nick.

“I bet it was the troll,” she said softly. Jenny cleaned up the dishes. She started the dishwasher. She helped Nick pack his bag. Soon the kids were ready to leave.

“We’re going to the bus stop,” called Jenny.

Ellen came to the door. "The car is fixed," said Ellen. "It was a loose wire. The man didn't know why. Have a good day at school. I'm off to my art show."

Ellen's art show is called "Animals in Pantyhose"

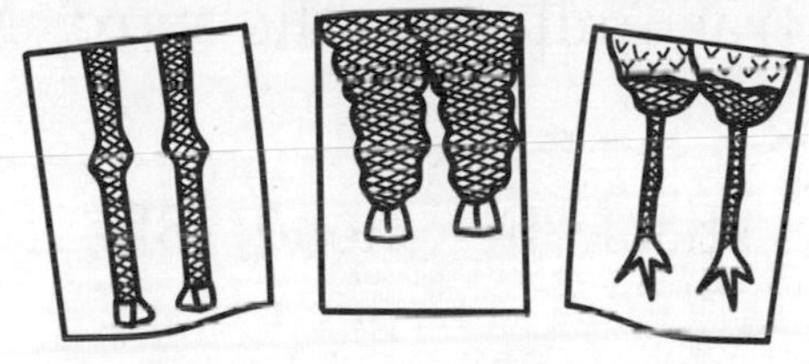

The kids walked to the bus stop.

"It was the troll," said Jenny. "The troll is making trouble."

"Why?" said Nick. "Why would he do that?"

"Because of my wish," said Jenny. She told Nick about her wish for Ellen.

"I don't know," said Nick. "Maybe."

After school Nick changed his mind.

The kids got off the bus. They saw Ellen in the yard. She was picking up trash. Lots of trash.

"What happened?" asked Jenny.

"I don't know," said Ellen. "I came home. I found trash all over the yard. Maybe it was a dog."

Jenny shook her head. She turned to Nick.

"Do you believe me now?" Jenny asked softly. "The freezer, the car, and now the trash. The troll is doing this. We have to stop him!"

5
NOT ME

Jenny looked at Ellen. Ellen shouldn't be picking up trash. Jenny should do it. Jenny made the bad wish.

"I'll pick up the trash," said Jenny.

"Thank you," said Ellen. "I'll start cooking dinner."

After dinner, Dad spoke to Jenny.

"Ellen told me about the car," he said. "And she told me about the trash."

"Yes," said Jenny. What was Dad going to say?

"I know you don't like Ellen," said Dad. "But I need to ask. Did you throw the trash around the yard?"

"No," said Jenny. "I didn't."

"Then how did the trash get all over the lawn? How did the trash cans get back by the house?" asked Dad.

Jenny looked at Dad. She couldn't tell him about the troll. He wouldn't believe her.

"I don't know," said Jenny. "But I did put the cans at the curb."

"What about the car?" asked Dad. "Do you know anything about the car?"

Jenny was surprised. Why would she know about the car?

"No," said Jenny. "I don't."

Jenny was upset. She went to her room. Nick came in.

"Does Dad think you made the trouble?" he asked. Jenny looked sad.

"Maybe," she said. "But what can I do? I can't tell him about my wish."

Nick was going to answer. But something happened. All the lights went off. The house was dark. There was no power.

"What has the troll done now?" asked Jenny. They heard Dad. He was in the kitchen talking to Ellen. The kids felt their way out of Jenny's room.

“I found it,” said Dad. “It was on the floor.” The lights came back on. The kids came in the kitchen.

“What happened?” asked Nick.

“It was a fuse,” said Dad. “A fuse came out. It was on the floor.”

“How can a fuse come out?” asked Nick.

“I don’t know,” said Dad. “Fuses don’t fall out. I think someone took it out.” Dad looked at Jenny. He looked sad.

“It wasn’t me,” yelled Jenny. “I didn’t do it. I didn’t do any of these things. Why won’t you believe me?” Jenny was mad. “I think

you don't love me anymore. I think you love Ellen more than me!"

"That's enough," said Dad. "Go to your room. We will talk later."

Jenny ran to her room. She slammed the door. She got on her bed. She put her face in her pillow.

After a little while, Ellen came in. She had a plate of cookies.

"I have some cookies for you," said Ellen.

Jenny didn't talk.

"I'm sorry Dad was mad," said Ellen. "He didn't mean it. He does love you."

Jenny kept her face in her pillow.

"I know you didn't do those things," said Ellen. "I know you didn't take out the freezer plug. Or the fuse. And I know you didn't throw trash on the lawn."

Jenny didn't move.

Soon Ellen left. Jenny lifted her face out of the pillow. She felt a little better. She sat up and ate the cookies.

6
ART STUDIO

It was Saturday. Dad and Ellen were going to an art show. Ellen hoped to sell some of her paintings. She put them in the car.

"We will be back after lunch," said Dad. "Have fun today." Then he and Ellen drove off. Nick turned to Jenny. He had his soccer ball.

“Will you come to the park with me?” he asked.

Jenny stared at Nick.

“What about the troll?” she asked. “We have to do something about the troll.”

“We can talk about it at the park,” said Nick. “Please kick with me. Then I will help you.”

Directions to the park

Jenny look upset. “I don’t want to wait,” she said. “But I don’t know what else to do. Let’s go.” The kids began to walk.

“Have you tried making another wish?” asked Nick.

"I did," said Jenny. "But it didn't work."

Nick and Jenny got to the park. They played soccer for a while. Soon they went home. Jenny checked on the troll.

"He's on the post," she told Nick.

The kids ate a snack. But then they heard a bump. And a crash.

"What was that?" asked Nick. The noises came from above. Nick and Jenny raced up the stairs. They looked in Ellen's studio.

"Oh no!" cried Jenny. Paint jars were knocked over. Brushes were on the floor. Papers were all over. All the paintings were off the walls. What would Ellen say?

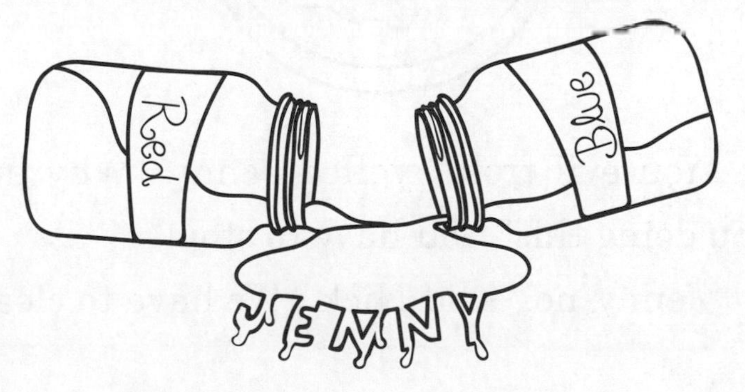

Then there were more bumps and crashes. The noises came from the kitchen. The kids raced back down the stairs. They ran into the kitchen.

"Oh no!" cried Jenny. Dirty dishes were on the table. Water was gushing in the sink. The trash can was tipped over. Jenny got mad. Really mad. She opened the back door.

"You evil troll!" yelled Jenny. "Why are you doing this? You have to stop!"

"Jenny, no," said Nick. "We have to clean

up. Dad and Ellen will be home soon." He pulled on Jenny's shirt. "I'll clean up the kitchen," he said. "You go up and work on Ellen's studio."

Jenny nodded. Nick was right. She went upstairs. She picked up the brushes. She picked up the jars of paint. Then she hung up the paintings. She hadn't seen these paintings before. This was Ellen's studio. Dad had asked the kids to stay out.

Ellen was a pretty good painter. Jenny picked up a painting of an old house. It looked nice. Why couldn't they live there? It looked charming. Wait! This was a painting of *their* house. Jenny hung the house painting up. How did Ellen make it look so nice?

Next was a painting of Nick. Ellen had done a great job. The Nick in the painting had the same messy hair as the real Nick.

He had the same goofy smile. Jenny hung Nick's picture up. Then she hung up other paintings. But the last painting made Jenny stop. It was a painting of her.

7
THE PAINTING

When had Ellen painted her? Jenny didn't know. She had never posed for Ellen.

Jenny stared at the painting. Ellen had painted her in her best outfit. It was the one she wore to the wedding. Her eyes looked deep brown. The freckles on her nose were just right. Her hair wasn't in a ponytail. It hung to her shoulders. It looked soft. And the Jenny in the painting was smiling. She was smiling in a happy way.

The real Jenny was surprised. How could Ellen paint her with a smile? Jenny didn't smile at Ellen. Not very often. Maybe she should. Ellen was a nice person. Jenny felt bad. She should smile more. She wanted Ellen to like her. But now the troll was messing things up. He was making it look like Jenny hated Ellen.

Jenny lifted the painting. She wanted to hang it on a nail. But the floor was bumpy. Jenny tripped. The painting slipped. It banged on the nail. The nail tore a hole. The hole was in Jenny's hair.

The real Jenny froze. How could such a bad thing happen? She was trying to help

Ellen. But now the painting was ripped. Ellen would be upset. Dad would be mad. He would say Jenny was being mean.

"Dumb floor!" yelled Jenny. A board was sticking up. She tried to stomp it down. It wouldn't go. Jenny kicked the board. It was loose. Jenny bent down. She took the board out. Now there was a hole in the floor.

Jenny saw something in the hole. It was a book. A small book was lying in the hole. Jenny reached in. She pulled out the book.

It looked very old. It was full of writing.

Jenny flipped some pages. Her eyes opened very wide. Nick had to see this book. He had to see it now.

Jenny raced down the stairs. Nick had cleaned up all the trash. He had put the dirty dishes in the dishwasher. The kitchen looked good.

Jenny pulled out a chair.

"Nick," said Jenny. "You have to look at this. Sit down and read this book with me. It's about the troll."

8
THE BOOK

Nick sat beside Jenny. She opened the book to the first page. She read the words aloud.

My name is Martha. I am ten years old. This is my secret book.

I must tell you what happened. Mother

and Father won't listen. Hannah won't listen. But maybe you will. Maybe you will find this book. Maybe my book will help you. My book can help you stop the troll.

"See," said Jenny. "I was right!"

"Keep reading," said Nick. Jenny turned the page.

I live in a big house with a big garden. The garden is full of roses. Around the garden is a stone wall. At one end is a gate.

On the gate's post sits a little stone troll. He looks grumpy. I think he looks funny.

Martha had drawn a picture in the book. It was the same troll. The troll that sat on the post. He was frowning. Jenny turned the page.

I have a little sister. Her name is Hannah. Hannah is cute. But sometimes she is bad.

One day she took my hat. My hat with the ribbons. I found it in the garden. It was muddy and ripped. I was very upset.

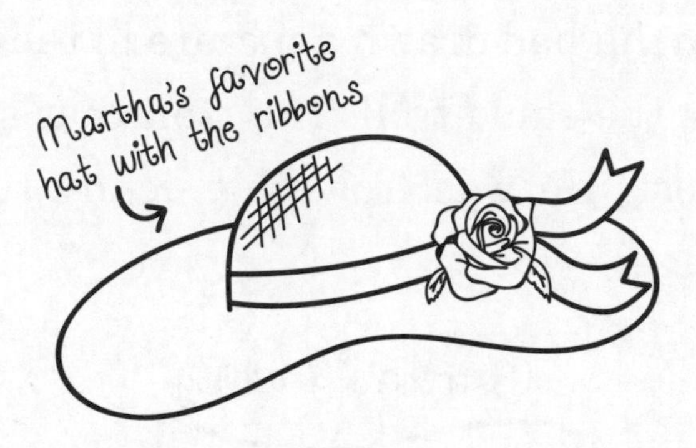

I told the troll about Hannah. I told him how mad I was. I liked talking to him. He always listened. He never talked back. I told him I wished Hannah would have bad luck.

That's when things started happening.

Jenny looked at Nick. He shook his head. Jenny turned the page.

First Hannah's hairbrush was gone.

Then her dress was torn. Then her slate was broken. No one knew how these things happened. Father asked me if I did it. He knew I was mad at Hannah. But I didn't do those things. It was the troll. He left the post. Then he came back. I knew he was granting my wish.

But a bad thing happened. Hannah fell down the stairs. She tripped. No one knows why. She hit her head. She was very hurt. The troll had gone too far. I had to stop him.

Jenny and Nick looked at each other. “This is bad,” said Jenny. “The troll is really bad.” She turned the page.

I went out to the garden. I had to stop the troll. But how? In the garden I met an old man. He said he was a wizard. He told me the troll's story.

Martha had drawn another picture. It was the wizard. He had a white beard. He wore a robe and a tall hat. He was looking at the troll. The troll had a nasty grin.

The wizard said the troll was evil. Long ago the wizard cast a spell. He turned the

troll into stone. But now the spell had ended. The troll was evil once more.

The wizard helped me stop him. The troll would never trouble Hannah again. But the wizard said one day his spell would end. Then the troll would make more trouble.

Have you made a wish? Was your wish mean? Has it come true? It's the troll. You must stop him. You have to undo your wish.

"But I tried," said Jenny. "It didn't work. What did I do wrong?"

"Turn the page," said Nick. "Turn the page and we'll find out." Jenny turned the page. Then she turned more pages.

"Oh no," said Jenny. "The rest of the book is blank."

9
THE WIZARD

"What good is this book?" said Jenny. "It didn't help us at all." She pushed the book away. Nick opened it. He started reading.

"There's no point," said Jenny. "There's nothing there. Dad is right. These bad things are my fault. I made the wish."

"There must be a clue," said Nick. "Martha said the book would help us."

But Jenny wasn't listening.

"I tried so hard to fix things," she said. "I picked up the paint. I hung up the paintings. Ugh! The painting. How can I tell Ellen about the rip?" Jenny put her head down on her hands.

"What rip?" asked Nick.

But Jenny wasn't listening. Then she sat up quickly.

"Give me the book," she said. "I have an idea." Nick slid the book across the table. Jenny turned to the second page. She stared at Martha's drawing. Then she turned to the other drawing. She put her eyes close to the book. Slowly a smile came to her face.

"Look," she said. She pointed at the stone post. She pointed at the side of the post. "Here's a clue."

"What is it?" asked Nick. He looked at

the drawing. There were tiny marks on the stone post. "Is it writing? I can't read it."

Jenny jumped up. "I'm going out to see," she said. She ran out to the garden. Nick followed.

The troll was gone.

"We have to hurry," yelled Jenny. "We have to stop him. Ellen will be home soon. The troll may do something very bad."

Jenny looked on the side of the post. She didn't see any writing. Just dead ivy vines.

"Help me pull these off," she said. Nick and Jenny ripped off the vines.

"Wait," yelled Jenny. "There it is." She could see letters. They looked old. They were hard to read.

"What is it?" asked Nick. "What does it say?"

Jenny peered at the letters.

"There are two words," she said. Jenny closed her eyes. She touched the words. She spoke them softly.

HELP ME

Warm air blew across her face. She smelled pepper. Then she heard a sneeze. Jenny opened her eyes. She looked at Nick. But he was staring at something else. Something behind Jenny.

There was another sneeze. Slowly Jenny turned around. Behind her was a man. He looked strange. He looked like a wizard!

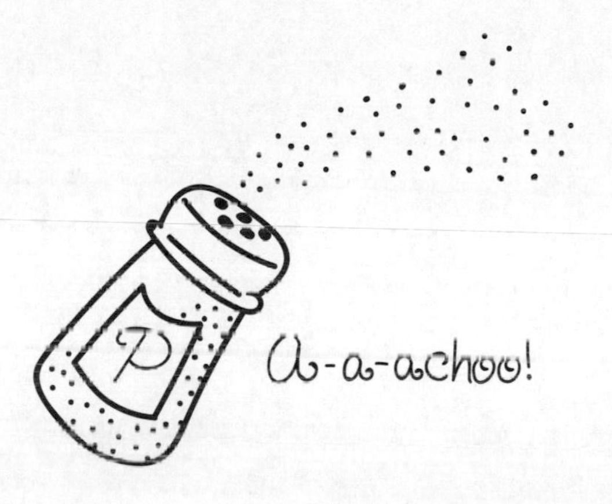

10
FRIENDS

Before Jenny could speak, she heard a new noise. It was the car. Dad and Ellen were home. They were home from the art show. Jenny turned to the wizard.

"Can you help me?" she begged. "I didn't mean to make my wish. I mean, I did

mean it then. But now I don't. I'm really sorry. Ellen has been trying so hard to be my friend."

She paused to breathe. "I haven't given her a chance. Not at all. I was kind of mean to her too. I don't want her to get hurt. I want to be her friend. I want the troll to stop."

Jenny's words came out fast. She was trying not to cry. Could this wizard help her? He wasn't even looking at her. He was rubbing his nose. Did he hear her? Maybe he was too old. Jenny tried again.

“Please,” Jenny said. “I really wish I could undo my wish.”

“Done,” said the wizard.

He pointed at the post. The garden troll was sitting there. He looked like he did before. He had that same grumpy frown on his face.

Jenny looked at the wizard in surprise.

“That’s it?” she said. “But that was so easy.”

“Was it?” asked the wizard. “Was it easy to say you’re sorry? Was it easy to say you had been mean.”

“I can say it now,” said Jenny. “But I

couldn't have said it before." The wizard nodded his head.

"Jenny! Nick! We're home." It was Ellen calling. The kids had to go inside. Jenny looked at the wizard. He gave her a wink. Jenny smiled. She turned and ran to the house.

Nick was still staring at the wizard. Nick hadn't moved. The wizard gave a little wave. He sneezed for a third time. Then he was gone. Nick slowly turned around. He walked to the house.

"I sold three paintings!" said Ellen when Jenny came in.

"That's great," said Jenny with a smile. She gave Ellen a hug. Ellen looked surprised.

"A man bought them," said Ellen. "He wants to put them in his office. He wants to buy more too." Jenny went with Ellen to the car.

"That's good news," said Jenny. "Can I help you unpack?"

"Sure," said Ellen. "You can carry these boxes. Your dad can get the paintings." Ellen handed two boxes to Jenny. Then Ellen lifted some more. They carried the boxes inside.

Jenny followed Ellen upstairs. She thought about the ripped painting. She wanted Ellen to be her friend. She wanted Ellen to trust her. She would have to tell

Ellen the truth. She would prove she was Ellen's friend. They walked into the studio.

"I have something to tell you," said Jenny. Jenny sounded sad. Ellen looked at her.

"I came in here today," said Jenny.

Ellen smiled. "That's okay," said Ellen. "You and Nick can come in any time."

"Yes, but I messed up something," said Jenny. She put down the boxes. She walked over to the painting. She looked up at herself. She gasped. The painting was perfect. Her hair was perfect. There was no rip.

"What did you mess up?" asked Ellen.

What could Jenny say? She couldn't tell Ellen about the rip now.

"Um. I saw this painting," Jenny said. "And I saw the painting of Nick. I think I messed up your surprise." Jenny hoped she had said the right thing.

"The paintings *were* a surprise," said Ellen. "But that's okay. I don't mind. I just want to know something. What do you think of them?"

"I like the one of Nick," said Jenny. "But I love the one of me."

"Really?" asked Ellen. "I wanted you to like it."

"I do," said Jenny. "In fact, can I ask you something? I was wondering … I mean … Do you think maybe you could teach me how to paint?"

"I'd love to," said Ellen. "Nothing would make me happier." She gave Jenny a big hug.

"Thanks, Ellen. And, Ellen? I'm glad you married my dad."

"Thank you, Jenny. That means a lot. I'll never be your mom. But I would like to be your friend. Okay?"

"Okay," said Jenny. "That sounds nice. I would like to be your friend too."